SARA
PARETSKY

A TASTE OF LIFE
AND OTHER STORIES

D0785802

PENGUIN BOOKS

PENGUIN BOOKS

Published by the Penguin Group. Penguin Books Ltd, 27 Wrights Lane, London w8 5tz, England. Penguin Books USA Inc., 375 Hudson Street, New York, New York 10014, USA. Penguin Books Australia Ltd, Ringwood, Victoria, Australia. Penguin Books Canada Ltd, 10 Alcorn Avenue, Toronto, Ontario, Canada m4v 3b2. Penguin Books (NZ) Ltd, 182–190 Wairau Road, Auckland 10, New Zealand · Penguin Books Ltd, Registered Offices: Harmondsworth, Middlesex, England · 'A Taste of Life' is taken from *Reader, I Murdered Him* (London, The Women's Press, 1989), 'Dealer's Choice' from *Raymond Chandler's Philip Marlowe* (New York, Knopf, 1988) and 'The Man Who Loved Life' from *New Chicago Stories* (Chicago, The City Stoop Press, 1990). This edition published 1995 · Copyright © Sara Paretsky, 1988, 1989, 1990. All rights reserved · The moral right of the author has been asserted · Typeset by Datix International Limited, Bungay, Suffolk. Printed in England by Clays Ltd, St Ives plc · Except in the United States of America, this book is sold subject to the condition that it shall not, by way of trade or otherwise, be lent, re-sold, hired out, or otherwise circulated without the publisher's prior consent in any form of binding or cover other than that in which it is published and without a similar condition including this condition being imposed on the subsequent purchaser · 10 9 8 7 6 5 4 3 2 1

CONTENTS

A Taste of Life   1

Dealer's Choice   11

The Man Who Loved Life   41

A Taste of Life

Daphne Raydor worked in the bookkeeping department at Rapelec, Inc. Her capacity for work – her appetite for it – was insatiable. In January, when accountants go mad closing previous years' books, Daphne flourished. She worked best in the night's dark hours, comparing ledgers and totting up columns with greedy delight.

Everyone at Rapelec loved Daphne in January. Helen Ellis, the petite, arrogant assistant controller, stopped to flatter Daphne on her plant arrangements or her perfume. Carlos Francetta, the budget director, lavished Latin compliments on her. Flowers appeared on her desk, and chocolates.

In February, these blandishments disappeared and Daphne lived alone behind her barricade of ferns for another eleven months. She was smart, she was willing, she was capable. But she was also very fat. She was so fat that she had to make all her own clothes: no store carried garments in her size. Her walk was slow. She gasped for breath after climbing a short flight of stairs. Daphne lived on the first floor of a three-storey walk-up. By the time she carried her groceries up one staircase and into her kitchen, she had to collapse for forty-five minutes to recover her breath.

Daphne was an excellent cook. She could make elaborate French dinners, including elegantly decorated pastries. Food and wine were both so outstanding that Helen, Carlos and other staff members would accept her dinner invitations. They would exclaim at their hostess, who barely touched her food: how could she be so fat, when she scarcely ate? After they left, Daphne would pull another four portions from the oven and devour them.

Daphne ate constantly. Elegant French dinners she reserved for company. She shopped almost daily, at five different supermarkets so that no one would see the volume of food she purchased. She had chocolate cookies tucked into a corner of the couch, bags of potato chips at her bedside and in the bathroom. The freezer and refrigerator were always overloaded. Some food rotted and had to be thrown out, but Daphne consumed a lot more. She brought home packages of frozen hors d'oeuvres and ate them while they thawed. She kept frozen pizzas under her bed and ate them raw. She slipped chocolates into drawers and closets. She was never more than three steps from some nourishing little snack.

Daphne's present condition was especially sad to those who knew her as an elfin child. What had happened to her? Family friends blamed Sylvia Raydor.

Twenty years ago, Sylvia's face appeared regularly on the covers of *Harper's Bazaar* and *Vogue*. She was one of the top ten models in the country and could pick her jobs. When Daphne was born, Sylvia delighted in the photographs – hovering sentimentally over a white-clad infant, blowing a sad kiss to baby and nurse from the railing of the *QE2* – that only enhanced her popularity.

But as Daphne moved from infant seats to kindergarten, she became an encumbrance to Sylvia. If the child was growing up, the mother must be ageing. And worse, friends – former friends – commented often on Daphne's angelic beauty. Photographers tried to bring her into the child-model business. Others prophesied a beauty that would far outshine Sylvia's, for it had a sweetness to it lacking in the mother.

Sylvia began force-feeding her daughter ('Mummy

won't love you if you don't eat all of this.' 'But Mummy, I'm not hungry!' 'Then Mummy will have to shut you in your room and leave you by yourself. She can't be with you if you hurt her feelings') until Daphne weighed close to 300 pounds.

As for Sylvia, she hardened into a still beautiful, if somewhat lacquered, jet-setter. She did a good business in television commercials (the housewife in the wildly successful Greazout detergent campaign) but was considered too brittle for magazines. She jetted to Minorca for the winter, spent spring in Paris, summered in the temperate zones off La Jolla, and generally alighted on Daphne's Chicago doorstep for a fleeting display of maternity in mid-October. ('Daphne, my pet! Darling, how *do* you manage to stay so fat? I eat and eat and can't put on an *ounce*!') Usually she had a young escort in tow, flattered by Sylvia's beauty and sophistication, yet contriving to make her appear a trifle old.

Daphne longed for love. She tried to satisfy her dreams with novels, beauty magazines (carefully cutting out Sylvia's face the few times it still appeared) and daydreams of an impossibly romantic character. And while she read, or dreamed of herself slim and desirable, she ate: a pound of pork chops with French fries, a chocolate layer cake and a quart of ice cream. And later a few pretzels and potato chips with beer. And so to bed.

One winter, a young man joined Rapelec's accounting department. He had a type of serious youthful beauty and was very shy. Daphne's fat, and her vulnerability, struck a responsive chord in Jerry. After thinking the matter over for several weeks, he waited until they were both alone at the end of the day and asked her to go to a movie with him. Daphne, whose dreams had been filled with Jerry's fine-etched features, at first thought he was making fun of her. But he persisted, and she finally agreed to go.

The first terrifying date took place in March. By May, Jerry and Daphne were lovers and Daphne had lost thirty-seven pounds. In September, she bought her first shop-made garment in eight years. A size twenty, to be sure, but a delirious occasion for her. In October, she and Jerry signed a lease together on Chicago's north side. That was where Sylvia found them some ten days later.

'Daphne, darling! Why didn't you let me know you were moving? I've searched everywhere for you, 5 and finally your genius of a secretary dug up your address for me!'

Daphne muttered something which a charitable listener could interpret as delight at seeing her mother. Sylvia eyed Jerry in a way which made him blush uncomfortably. 'Introduce me to your friend, darling,' she cried reproachfully. Daphne did so, reluctantly, and then muttered that they were going to paint cabinets, and didn't paint always make Syvia sick?

'You don't want to paint the first night your mother is in town,' Sylvia said archly, inviting Jerry to compare mother with daughter, indeed pausing for the expected remark ('You can't be her mother – if anything, she looks older than you!'). Jerry said nothing, but blushed more than ever.

'Why, you two babies,' Sylvia finally said. 'Anyone would think I'd found you out in some guilty secret. Instead, here you are setting up house in the most delightful way. Let's go over to Perroquet to celebrate!'

'Thanks, Sylvia, but I – I guess I'm not hungry and these cabinets do need painting.'

Sylvia cried out some more, drew the embarrassed

Jerry into the conversation – 'You must be making

this goose of a daughter perfectly *miserable*, Jerry: she's never lost her appetite in all the years I've known her' — and finally dragged them off to Perroquet where she ordered for all of them and pouted when Daphne refused several courses. 'If you were a model, darling, one could understand. But you can eat whatever you feel like.'

Back home, Daphne burst into tears. How could Jerry love her, as fat as she was, and why didn't Sylvia drop dead? Jerry consoled her, but uneasily. And Sylvia, back in her suite, Sylvia could not rest. Daphne happy and in love? Impossible. Daphne thin? Never!

Sylvia's courtship of Jerry was long and difficult. She postponed her winter plans and stayed in Chicago, hosting parties, making a splash at all the society events, getting Jerry to escort her when Prince Philip hosted a dress ball at the British consulate.

Daphne watched wretchedly, hopeless and unable to act. She began eating again, not at her previous levels, but enough to put ten pounds back on by Thanksgiving.

Jerry, too, was miserable and unable to cope with Sylvia. He dreaded her summonses, yet could not 7 refuse them. The night finally came when he did not return to the apartment.

Desolate, Daphne sat up in bed waiting for him. By three, it was clear that he wasn't coming home. She began to eat, consuming the roast she had prepared for their dinner and what little other food they had – for her sake they didn't stock much.

As soon as the stores were open, Daphne went to the nearest grocery and bought as much as she could carry. Returning home, she dropped two heavy sacks in the middle of the living room and sat down to eat. She did not take off her coat, nor bother to call her office. She ate a dozen sweet rolls, a cherry pie, and two pizzas. She was working her way through a box of chips with dip when Sylvia appeared.

Sylvia stopped in the middle of the room. 'What on earth are you doing here? I was sure you would be at work!'

Daphne got clumsily to her feet. She looked at Sylvia, furiously angry, yet feeling passive and remote. She wanted to cry, to eat a pound of chocolates, to throw Sylvia out the window, yet she only stood. Finally she spoke. Her voice sounded so far away that she wondered if she'd said the words aloud and repeated herself. 'What are you doing here, Sylvia? Get out.'

Sylvia laughed. 'Oh, I came to get Jerry's clothes – he didn't want to come himself – felt awkward, poor thing.'

Daphne followed her into the bedroom. 'You can't have Jerry's clothes,' she whispered. 'I want them myself.'

'Oh, do be reasonable, Daphne: Jerry won't be coming back. Why he ever wanted a fat lump like you I don't know, but at least it gave me a chance to meet him, so I suppose it was all to the good.' As she spoke, Sylvia began pulling drawers open, impatiently pawing through jeans and T-shirts.

'You can't take his clothes,' Daphne whispered hoarsely, pulling at Sylvia's arm.

'Buzz off now, Daphne, and finish your cookies,' Sylvia snapped, slapping her across the face.

Daphne screamed in rage. Scarcely knowing what she was doing, she picked up the dressing-table lamp and began pounding Sylvia's head with it. Sylvia fell against the dressing-table and at last lay crumpled on the floor, dead long before Daphne stopped screaming and hitting her.

Finally Daphne's rage subsided. She collapsed on

the floor by Sylvia's body and began to cry. Jerry would never come back to her. No one would ever love her again. She wanted to die herself, to eat and eat until she was engulfed by food. Mechanically, methodically, still weeping, she lifted Sylvia's left arm to her mouth.

Dealer's Choice

1942

She was waiting in the outer office when I came in, sitting with a stillness that made you think she'd been planted there for a decade or two and could make it to the twenty-first century if she had to. She didn't move when I came in except to flick a glance at me under the veil of the little red hat that had built a nest in her shiny black hair. She was all in red; she'd taken the May's company's advertisers to heart and was wearing victory red. But I doubted if she'd ever seen the inside of May's. This was the kind of shantung number that some sales clerk acting like the undertaker for George V pulled from a back room and whispered to madam that it might suit if madam would condescend to try it on. The shoes and gloves and bag were black.

'Mr Marlowe?' Her voice was soft and husky with a hint of a lisp behind it.

I acknowledged the fact.

She got to her feet. Perched on top of her boxy four-inch heels she just about cleared my armpit.

'I've been hoping to see you, Mr Marlowe. Hoping to interest you in taking a case for me. If you have the time, that is.'

She made it sound as though her problem, whatever it was, was just a bit on the dull side, and that if I didn't have time for it the two of us could forget it and move on to something more interesting. I grunted and unlocked the inner door. The muffled tapping on the rug behind me let me know she was following me in.

The April sunshine was picking up the dust motes dancing on the edge of my desk. I dumped the morning paper on to the blotter and reached into my desk drawer for my pipe. My visitor settled herself in the other chair with the same composure she'd shown in the outer office. Whatever little problem she had didn't make her twitch or catch her heels in her rosy silk stockings.

While I was busy with my pipe she leaned forward in her chair, looking at the paper; something on the front page had caught her eye. Maybe the Red Army bashing the Krauts along the Caspian, or the US carving a few inches out of Milne Bay. Or Ichuro Kimura eluding the US Army right here at home, or 12 maybe the lady whose twin daughters were celebrating their first birthday without ever having seen their daddy. He was interned by the Japs in Chungking.

When she caught me watching her she settled back in her chair. 'Do you think the war will end soon, Mr Marlowe?'

'Sure,' I said, tamping the tobacco in. 'Out of the trenches by Christmas.' We'd missed Easter by a day already.

The girl nodded slightly to herself, as if I'd confirmed her opinion of the war. Or maybe me. The bright sunlight let me see her eyes now, despite the little veil. The irises were large and dark, looking black against the clear whites. She was watching me calmly enough but those eyes gave her away – they could light up the whole Trojan backfield if she wanted to use them that way. But something in her manner and that hint of a lisp made me think they didn't play much football where she came from.

'I need some help with a man,' she finally said.

'You look as though you do just fine without help.' I struck a match against the side of the desk.

She ignored me. 'He's holding some of my brother's markers.'

'Your brother lose them in fair play?'

She gave me a shrug that moved like a whisper through the shantung. 'I wouldn't know, Mr Marlowe. All I know is that my brother staked a – an item that didn't belong to him. My brother has gone into hiding, since he knows he can't pay up and he's afraid they'll break his legs, or whatever it is they do when you can't pay your gambling losses.'

'Then I don't see you have a problem. All you have to do is keep supplying your brother with food and water and everyone will be happy. Your gambler will go after easier prey by and by. What's his name?'

I thought I saw a faint blush, but it was such a phantom wave of color I couldn't be sure. It made me think she knew where her brother was all right.

'Dominick Bognavich. And if it were just my brother I wouldn't mind, not so much I mean, since he was gambling and he has to take his chances. But they're threatening my mother. And that's where I need your help. I thought perhaps you could explain to Mr Bognavich – get him to see that – he should leave my mother alone.'

I busied myself with my pipe again. 'Your brother shouldn't bet with Bognavich unless he can stake the San Joaquin Valley. I believe that's all Dominick doesn't own at this point. What did your brother put up?'

She watched me consideringly. I knew that look. It was the kind I used when I wondered if a chinook would accept my bait.

'A ring,' she finally said. 'An old diamond and sapphire ring that had been in Mother's family for a hundred years. My brother knows he'll get it when she's dead, and she could die tomorrow – I don't know – she's very ill and in a nursing home. So he anticipated events.'

Anticipated events. I like that. It showed a certain thoughtfulness with the language and the people. 'And what about your brother? I mean, does he have a name, or do we do this whole thing incognito?'

She studied me again. 'No, I can see you need his name. It's – uh – Richard.'

'Is that his first or his last name? And do you have the same last name or should I call you something else?'

'You can call me Miss Felstein. Naomi Felstein. And that would be Richard's last name, too.'

'And your mother is Mrs Felstein, and your father is Mr Felstein.'

'Was.' She gave a tight little smile, the first I'd 15

seen and not any real sample of what she could do if she were in the mood. 'He's been dead for some years now.'

'And what is it you want me to do for you, Miss Felstein? Shoot Dominick Bognavich? He's got a lot of backups and I might run out of bullets before he ran out of people to send after me.'

One black-gloved finger traced a circle on the arm of the chair. 'Maybe you could see Mr Bognavich and explain to him. About my brother not owning the ring, I mean. Or – or maybe you could talk my brother into coming out of hiding. He won't listen to me.'

Sure I could talk to Bognavich. He and I were good pals, sure we were, and my words carried a lot of weight with him, about as much as maggots listening to protests from a dead body. I didn't like it, any of it. I didn't believe her story and I didn't believe in her brother. I was pretty sure she didn't have a brother, or if she did Bognavich had never heard of him. But it was the day after Easter and I'd been too savvy to let myself get suckered by the Easter bunny, so I owed the rubes one.

I gave her my usual rate, twenty-five dollars a day and expenses, and told her I'd need some up-front money. She opened the little black bag without a word and lifted ten twenties from a stash in the zipper compartment with the ease of a dealer sliding off queens to send you over the top in twenty-one.

She gave another ghostly smile. 'I'll wait for you here. In case you have no success with Mr Bognavich and want me to take you to my brother.'

'I'll call you, Miss Felstein.'

That seemed to confuse her a little. 'I may – I don't –'

'I'd rather you didn't wait in my office. I'll call you.'

Reluctantly she wrote a number on a piece of paper and handed it to me. Her script was bold and dark, the writing of a risk taker. Oh, yeah, her brother lost some big ones to Dominick Bognavich all right.

A guy like Bognavich doesn't start his rounds until the regular working stiffs are heading home for a drink. If I was lucky I'd make it to his place before he went to bed for the day. But when I'd wound my way up Laurel Canyon to Ventura, where Bognavich had a modest mansion on a cul-de-sac, I found he'd

17

become the kind of guy who doesn't make rounds any time of day.

He was slumped against the door leading from the garage to the house. He looked as though he'd felt tired getting out of the car and decided to sit down for a minute to catch his breath but had fallen asleep instead. It was just that he had taken the kind of nap where six small-caliber bullets give you a permanent hangover.

I felt his face and wrists. He'd been dead for a while; if I had a look around without calling the cops it wasn't going to halt the wheels of justice any. The door behind him was unlocked, an invitation for fools to go dancing in and chase the angels out. I listened for a while but didn't hear anything, not even Dominick's blood congealing on the floor.

The kitchen was a white-tiled affair that looked like the morgue after a good scrubdown. I gave it a quick once-over, but Bognavich wasn't the kind of guy who hid his secrets in the granulated sugar. I passed on through to the main part of the house.

The gambler had employed a hell of a housekeeper. She'd left sofa cushions torn apart with their stuffing spread all over the pale gold on the living-room floor. White tufts clung to my trouser legs like cottontails.

Marlowe the Easter bunny hunting for eggs the other kids hadn't been able to find.

Bognavich's study was where he'd kept his papers. He'd been a gambler, not a reader, and most of the books dealt with the finer points of cards and horses. They lay every which way, their backs breaking, loose pages lying nearby like pups trying to get close enough to suckle their dam.

I did the best I could with the papers and the ledger. There were IOUs for the asking if I'd been inclined to go hustling for bread, but nothing that looked like a Felstein. I didn't feel like lingering for a detailed search. Whoever had put those six holes into Dominick might be happy for the cops to find an unwelcome peeper fingering the gambler's papers. I gave the rest of the house a quick tour, admired Bognavich's taste in silk pajamas, and slid back through the kitchen.

He was still sitting where I'd left him. He seemed to sigh as I passed. I patted him on the shoulder and went back to the Chrysler. Miss Felstein could have put six rounds into Bognavich without wrinkling her silk dress, let alone her smooth little forehead. It was the kind of shooting a dame might do — six bullets where one or two would do the job. Wasteful, with a war on.

I pulled the pint from the glove compartment and swallowed a mouthful just on principle, a farewell salute to Dominick. He hadn't been a bad guy, he just had a lousy job.

I half expected to find Miss Naomi Felstein, if that was who she was, not just what I could call her, planted in my waiting room like a well-kept jacaranda. I expected her because I wanted her to be there. I wanted to see if I could shake a little fire into those cool dark eyes and get her to tell me why she'd come to me after finding Dominick's dead body lying in front of his kitchen door this morning.

She wasn't there, though. I wondered if she ever had been there, if perhaps she was just an Easter vision, in red the way these visions always appear, leaving the faintest whiff of Chanel behind to undercut the tobacco fumes. I had a drink from the office bottle and the Chanel disappeared.

I didn't have much hope for the number the mirage had left, and my hope began to dwindle after fifteen rings. But I didn't have anything else to do so I sat at my desk with the phone in my ear looking at the front page of the paper, trying again to figure out which of the stories had caught my phantom's attention.

I finished the details of Errol Flynn's cruelty to

his wife and why she had to get his entire estate as a settlement and started on why the army thought Ichuro Kimura was an enemy spy. I'd gotten to the part where he'd thrown empty sake bottles at the soldiers who came to arrest him for not reporting for deportation at Union Station last Wednesday when I realized someone was talking to me.

It was a querulous old man who repeated that he was the Boylston Ranch and who was I calling. Without much interest I asked for Miss Felstein.

'No one here by that name. No women here at all.' His tone demanded congratulations for having rid Eden of all temptresses.

'Five feet tall, lots of glossy black hair, dark eyes that could bring a guy back from the grave if she wanted them to.'

He hung up on me. Just like that. I stuck the bottle of rye neatly in the middle of the drawer and stared at nothing for a while. Then I got up and locked the office behind me. Oh, yes, Marlowe's a very methodical guy. Very orderly. He always tidies up his whisky bottle when he's been drinking and locks up behind himself. You can tell he came from a good home.

The army had a roadblock set up just outside Lebec. I guess they were trying to make sure no one was smuggling empty sake bottles in for Ichuro Kimura. They made me get out of my car while they looked under the seats and in the trunk. Then they checked my ID and made me tell them I was looking for a runaway girl and that I had a hot tip she was hiding out on the Boylston place. That made them about as happy as a housewife seeing her cat drag a dead bird into the kitchen. They started putting me through my paces until the sergeant who was running the block came over and told them to let me through. He was bored: he wanted to be killing Japs at Milne Bay instead of looking for old men in Lebec.

The sun had had all it could take of Kern County by the time I got to the turnoff for the Boylston Ranch. It was easing itself down behind the Sierra Madres, striking lightning bolts from the dashboard that made it hard for me to see. I was craning my neck forward, shielding my eyes with my left hand, when I realized I was about to go nose to nose with a pickup.

I pulled over to the side to let the truck go by, but it stopped and a lean, dusty man jumped down. He had on a cowboy hat and leather leggings, in case the gearshift chafed his legs, and his face was young and angry, with a jutting upper lip trying to dominate the uncertain jaw beneath it.

'Private property here, mister. You got any reason to be here?'

'Yup,' I said.

'Then let's have it.'

I got out of the Chrysler to be on eye level with him, just in case being alone with the cows all day made him punch happy.

'You got any special reason for asking, son? Other than just nosiness, I mean?'

His fists clenched reflexively and he took half a step nearer. 'I'm Jay Boylston. That good enough for you?'

'You own this spread?'

'My old man does, but I'm in charge of the range. So spill it, and make it fast. Time is money here and I don't have much to waste of either.'

'An original sentiment. Maybe you could get it engraved on your tombstone. If your old man owns the place I'd better talk to him. It's kind of a delicate matter. Involves a lady's reputation, you might say.'

At that he did try to swing at me. I grabbed his arm. It was a bit tougher than his face but not much.

'What's going on here?'

The newcomer had ridden up behind us on horseback. The horse stopped in its tracks at a short command and the rider jumped down. He was an older, stockier edition of Jay. His face held the kind of arrogance men acquire when they own a big piece of land and think it means they own all the people around them as well.

'Man's trespassing and he's giving kind of smart answers when I ask him to explain himself,' Jay said sullenly.

'Mr Boylston?' I asked. The older man nodded fractionally, too calm to give anything to a stranger, even the movement of his head.

'Philip Marlowe. I'm a private detective from Los Angeles and I'm up here on a case.'

'A case involving my ranch is something I would know about,' Boylston said. His manner was genial but his eyes were cold.

'I didn't say it involved your ranch. Except as a hiding place for a runaway. Big place, lots of places to hide. Am I right?'

'The army's been all through here in the last week looking for a runaway Jap,' Boylston said. 'I don't think there's too much those boys missed. You're a long way from LA if you hope to sleep in your own bed tonight.'

'This is a recent case,' I said doggedly, Marlowe the intrepid, fighting on where others would have turned tail and run. 'This is a woman who only recently disappeared. And she's attractive enough that someone might be persuaded to hide her from the army.'

Boylston had headed back to his horse, but at the end of my speech he turned back to me. He exchanged a glance with his son. When Jay shook his head the father said, 'Who's the girl?'

'I don't have a name. But she's five feet tall, glossy black hair, probably a lot of it but she wears it in kind of a roll or chignon or whatever they're calling them this year. Very well dressed – lots of money in the background someplace.'

'If you don't know her name how do you know she's missing or even what she looks like?'

I smiled a little. 'I can't tell you all my secrets, Mr Boylston. But I will tell you she's wanted for questioning about a murder down in LA.'

Boylston swung himself back onto his horse. 'I haven't seen anyone like that. I can account for all the women around here: my two daughters, and 25 three of the hands are married, and none of 'em has black hair. But if you want to look around, be my guest. There's an abandoned farmhouse on up the road about five miles. We just acquired the land so we only have one hand living out there so far; he can't keep an eye on the house and cover the range, too. That'd be the only place I know of. If you don't see her there you'd best get off my land. Now move your truck, Jay, and let Mr Marlowe get by.'

Jay got into the truck and moved it with an ill will that knocked little pebbles into the side of the Chrysler. I climbed back in and headed on up the track. In the rearview mirror I could see Boylston on his horse watching me, standing so still he might have been a knight on a chessboard.

The road petered out for a while into a couple of tire marks in the grass, but after four miles it turned into a regular road again. Not too long after that I came to the house.

It was a single-story, trim ranch, built like a U with short arms. It was made of wood and painted white, fresh as the snow on the Sierras, with green trim like pine trees. Whoever used to live here had loved the place and kept it up. Or the hand who was watchdogging was a homebody who kept the shrubs trimmed and weeded the begonias.

I rang the bell set into the front door, waited a few minutes, and rang again. It was sunset, not too unreasonable to think the man was done with his chores for the day. But he might be in the shower and not able to hear me ringing. I tried the door and found it unlocked. I pushed it open and went on in with a cloud of virtue wrapped around my shoulders. After all, I wasn't even housebreaking – I had Boylston's permission to search the place.

The hall floor was tiled in brown ceramic with a couple of knotted rugs floating on it. The tiles were covered with a film of dust – the hand who lived there didn't have time for the finer points of housekeeping. Opposite the front door, sliding glass doors led to a garden, a place which the previous owner had tended with care. I stared through the glass at the trim miniature shrubs and flowering bushes. There even seemed to be a pond in the middle.

I turned left and found myself in the kitchen wing. No one was hiding in the stove or under the sink. The other wing held the bedrooms. In one you could see the cowboy's obvious presence, several pairs of jeans, a change of boots, another of regular 27 shoes. The other two bedrooms had been stripped of their furnishings. No one was in the closets or hiding in the two bathtubs.

The only thing that gave me hope was the telephone. It sat next to the kitchen stove, and pasted to it, in neat printing, not my mirage's bold script, was the number I had called. The number where the querulous man had hung up on me after I'd described her.

When I'd finished with the bedrooms I went back to the sliding door leading into the small garden. Sure enough, a pool stood in the middle, bigger than it had appeared from inside the house. I climbed on to a bridge that crossed it and looked down. Immediately a trio of giant goldfish popped to the surface. They practically stood on their tails begging for bread.

'Go work for a living like the regular fish,' I admonished them. 'There's a war on. No one has time to pamper goldfish.'

The fish swam under the bridge. I turned and looked down at them. They'd taken my words to heart – they were hard at work on the face and hands of a man who was staring up at me in the shallow water. In the fading light I couldn't make out his features, but he still had all of them so he couldn't have been in the water long. His dark hair waved like silk seaweed in the little eddies the carp stirred up.

What a detective that Marlowe is. Someone strews bodies all over Southern California and Marlowe finds them with the ease and derring-do of a bloodhound. I wanted a flashlight so I could get a closer look at the face. I wanted a drink and a cigarette, and I was beginning to think I shouldn't stray too far from my gun. All these useful items were in the Chrysler's glove compartment. I headed back through the house, skating on the lily pads on the tile floor, and climbed into the passenger seat. I had just unscrewed the bottle cap when I detected something else – a grand display of pyrotechnics exploding in my retinas. I didn't even feel the blow, just saw the red stabbing lights riding on a wave of nausea before I fell into deep blackness.

My head was a seventy-eight on a turntable that had automatic reset. Every time I thought I'd come to the end of the song and could stop spinning around someone would push the button and start me turning again. Someone had tied a couple of logs behind my back but when I reached around to cut them loose I discovered they were my arms bound behind me. I reeked of gasoline.

The time had come to open my eyes. Come on, Marlowe, you can get your eyelids up, it's only a little less horrible than the old bamboo shoots under the fingernails trick.

I was in the driver's seat of the Chrysler. Someone had moved me over, but otherwise the scene was just the way I'd left it. The glove compartment was open. I could see my gun and the bottle of rye and I wanted both of them in the kind of detached fashion a man lost in the desert wants an oasis, but I couldn't see my way clear to getting them.

Footsteps scrabbled on the gravel behind me. 'You can't set fire to him here,' someone said impatiently. 'You may own the valley, but the US Army is camped on the road and they will certainly investigate a big gasoline fire up here.'

I knew that voice. It was husky, with a hint of lisp behind it. I'd heard it a century or so ago in my office.

'Well, you're such a damned know-it-all, what do you suggest? That we leave him here until morning when the hands will find him?' The sulky tones of the kid, Jay Boylston.

'No,' the woman said coolly, 'I think you should let me drive him into the mountains. He can go over a ravine there and no one will be surprised.'

'Kitty's right,' Boylston senior said authoritatively.

Kitty? She was a kitty all right, the kind that you usually like a good solid set of iron bars around before you toss raw meat to her twice a day. There was a bit more backchat about who would do the driving, but they agreed in the end that the kitten could do it so that no one would wonder where Jay and his daddy were.

'You fired his gun?' Daddy asked.

'Yes,' Jay said sulkily. 'I shot Richard twice with it. When they find him they'll think Marlowe did it.'

'Right. Kitty, just see that his gun falls clear of the car before you set it off. We want to make sure the law doesn't have any loose ends to tie up.'

So she did have a brother named Richard. Or had had. That wavy black hair in the goldfish pond, that was what her dark leopard tresses would look like if she undid that bun.

'Sure, Kurt,' the husky voice drawled.

Kurt and Jay shoved me roughly back into the passenger seat and Miss Kitty took my spot behind the wheel. I tried to sniff the Chanel, but the gasoline fumes were too strong. She drove rapidly up the track, bouncing the Chrysler's tires from rock to rock as though she was driving a mountain goat.

Things looked bad for Marlowe. I wondered if it was worth trying any of my winsome charms, or if I should just roll over on top of her and force both of us flaming into a ditch. It was worth a try. At least it would change the situation – give those cool black eyes something to look surprised about. I was getting ready to roll when she stopped the car.

Her next move took me utterly by surprise: she reached behind me and hacked my arms loose with an efficient woodsman's knife.

'You're kind of pushing your luck, Kitty.' I moved my arms cautiously in front of me. They felt like someone had just forced the Grand Coulee's overflow through them. 'I've been concussed before. I'm not feeling so sorry for myself that I couldn't take that knife from you and get myself out of here. You'd have to explain it to Kurt and Jay as best you can.'

'Yes,' the husky voice agreed coolly. 'I'll tell them something if I have to – if I ever see them again, that is. But I need your help.'

'Right, Miss Kitty. You lure me to Dominick

Bognavich's body. You bring me into the mountains and set the sweetest sucker trap I've ever seen, including planting bullets from my gun in what I assume is your brother's body, and now you want my help. You want me to drive my car over a cliff for you so you don't have to chip those bright red nails of yours?'

She drew a sharp breath. 'No. No. I didn't know they were going to knock you out. And I didn't know they had killed Richard until I got here. He – he was the weak link. He always was, but I never thought he would betray me.'

The quiver of emotion in her voice played on my heart like a thousand violin strings. 'The gambler. I know. He gambled away your mother's whoosis and so you had Kurt Boylston drown him in the goldfish pond.'

'It didn't happen quite like that. But I don't blame you for being angry.'

'Gee, sister. That's real swell of you. I'm not angry, though – I love being hit on the head. I came up from LA just to get knocked out. And then have gasoline poured on me so I couldn't miss the cars.'

'That was never supposed to happen,' she said quickly. 'I was trying to get to Grandfather – to the 33 ranch – before Jay did but I couldn't – there were reasons . . .' Her voice trailed away.

'Maybe you could tell me what was supposed to happen. If it wouldn't strain your brain too much to tell the truth. Maybe you could even start with who you really are.'

In the dark I couldn't tell if she was blushing or not. 'My real name is Kathleen Moloney. Kathleen Akiko Moloney. My mother married an Irishman, but her father was Ichuro Kimura. I know I look Jewish to many people and in this climate today it is helpful to let them think so. Dominick – Dominick is the one who suggested it. He suggested the name Felstein. And when I pretended to lose the title to my grandfather's land to him, he kept it under the name of Felstein.' Her voice trailed away. 'I needed help and I was so afraid you wouldn't help me . . .'

'If I knew you were Nisei.' I finished for her. 'And what makes you so sure I will help you now?'

'I don't know.' She leaned close to me and I could smell her perfume again, mixed with the gasoline and a faint tinge of ladylike sweat. 'I saved your life, but that wouldn't count with you, would it, if you thought it was your duty to turn me in and force me to go to Manzanar.'

'You're not in any danger. A girl like you knows how to fight her way out of trouble.'

'Yes. I have to use the gifts I have, just as you do, Mr Marlowe. But we can argue about that later. Let me finish because we must move quickly. If you agree to help me, I mean.'

In the moonlight all I could see was her shape. She'd shed the hat and the suit and was wearing trousers and cowboy boots. I couldn't see her features to tell if she was spinning me another long yarn into which she had somehow appropriated the tale of Ichuro Kimura from the morning paper. I shook a large portion of rye into me to give my brain a fighting edge.

'Don't drink,' she said sharply to me. 'It's the worst thing for a man in your condition.'

'On the contrary,' I said, tilting the bottle a second time. The first swallow had settled the nausea in my stomach and sharpened the pain in my head, but the second one went clear to the base of my spine and worked its way into the brain. 'I think I can stand to hear your tale of woe now. Tell me about Richard, the weakling.'

'Kurt Boylston has wanted to own my grandfather's land for a long time. It's a small ranch, only 35

nine hundred acres, nothing compared to the Boylston spread, but it has the best water. My grandfather
worked it as a field hand when he came here from
Japan in 1879 and gradually came to own it.

'Boylston has tried everything to get his hands on
it. Then, with the internments and the anti–Japanese
scare, he saw his chance. He announced that Kimura
was a Japanese spy and that his land should be
confiscated. Boylston said he would farm it as a
service to the government. Of course, in times like
these, frightened men will believe anything.'

Her husky voice was shaky with passion. I wanted
a cigarette very badly but didn't want to send us up
in flames lighting it.

'My grandfather would not go. Why should he?
He is no spy. And he knew it was only a ruse, a trick
by Kurt Boylston to get his land. I'm sure you saw
in the paper how he fought the army and then
disappeared. I took the title and gave it to Dominick,
but I had to tell Richard. And Richard was weak.
Kurt must have bought him. I saw – I saw when I
got to Dominick's house this morning, how he had
been shot, and knew it was Richard, shooting him
six times out of fright, then tearing the house up to
36 find the title. After he turned it over to Kurt, the

Boylstons drowned him in my grandfather's goldfish pond. I pretended all along to be in love with Kurt, to be supporting him against my grandfather, but after tonight even he will be able to understand.'

I wondered if even now she was telling the truth. She sure believed in it, but did I? 'Why didn't you tell me this this morning?'

The moonlight caught leopard sparks dancing from her eyes. 'I didn't think you'd believe me. A Japanese spy, written up in all the papers? I thought I would get here ahead of you and explain it all to you, but then I saw Richard's body in the pond and knew that Kurt would figure out my true involvement before long. I had – had to go back to his ranch and –' Her voice broke off as she shuddered. 'I used my special gifts, that's all, and took the title from his pocket while he slept.'

I put one of my gasoline-soaked hands on her soft leopard paw. Why not? She'd told a good tale, she deserved a little applause.

'Bravo. You got your paper back. You don't need me. You want a lift someplace on my way back to LA?'

She sucked her breath in again and pulled her hand back. 'I do need you. To smuggle my grandfather into the city. The army knows my car, and they know my face. They would stop me, but they won't stop you.'

I rubbed the bottle a few times, wondering if her grandfather would pop out of it, a wizened Japanese genie.

'He's been hiding here in an old well, but it's bad for him, bad for his rheumatism, and it's hard for me to sneak him food. And now, he could climb down into the well, but not up, not by himself, but you – you are strong enough for two.'

She was the genie in the bottle, or maybe she just had a little witch blood mixed in with the leopard. I found myself walking across the jagged ground to where a well cover lay hidden beneath the sage. I pried it loose according to the enchantress's whispered instructions. She knelt down on the rim and called softly, 'It's Akiko, Grandfather. Akiko and a friend who will bring you to Los Angeles.'

It wasn't as simple as Miss Moloney thought it would be, driving around to pick up Route Five from the north, but then these things never are. In the first place Kimura wouldn't travel without a little shrine to the Buddha that he'd been keeping in the well with him, and it was a job packing the two of them in the trunk under some old blankets. And in the second place we ran into Kurt and Jay because the only way to Route Five was along the trail that led past the Kimura place. And in the confusion I put a bullet through Kurt Boylston's head – purely by mistake, as I explained to the sheriff, but Miss Moloney had hired me to look for rustlers on her grandfather's old place and when Kurt had started to shoot at us I didn't know what else to do. The sheriff liked it about as well as a three-day hangover, but he bought it in the end.

What with one thing and another the sun was poking red fingers up over the San Gabriels by the time we coasted past Burbank and into the city.

I dropped Miss Moloney and her grandfather at a little place she owned in Beverly Hills, just ten rooms and a pool in the back. I figured Dominick had been a pretty good friend, all right. Or maybe the Irishman who married her mother – I was willing to keep an open mind.

She invited me in for a drink, but I didn't think gasoline and rye went too well with the neighborhood or the decor, so I just left the two of them to the ministrations of a tearful Japanese maid and lowered myself by degrees through the canyons back to the 39 city. The concrete looked good to me. Even the leftover drunks lying on the park benches looked pretty good. I've never been much of an outdoors man.

When I got to my office I tried the air to see if there was any perfume left, but I couldn't detect it. I wondered what kind of detective I was, anyway. There wasn't anything for me in the office. I didn't know why I'd come here instead of finding my shower and bed – that was the kind of thing I could detect all right.

I put the office bottle back in the drawer and locked it. I put yesterday's paper tidily in the trash can and looked around for a minute. There was a scrap of black on the floor underneath the visitor's chair. I bent over to pick it up. It was a little square of lace, the kind of thing a lady with the poise of a dealer would have tucked in her black bag, the kind of thing even the most sophisticated lady might drop when she was peeling off twenties. It smelled faintly of Chanel. I put it in my breast pocket and locked the door.

The Man Who Loved Life

Simon Peter Dresser looked down at the long rows of tables. Pride made his heart grow in his chest, pressing against his throat so that he could hardly respond to the bishop sitting on his right. If only his daddy could see him now, bishops deferring to him, politicians courting him and hundreds of people looking up to where he sat at the center of the head table, admiration glowing from their faces.

His daddy had snorted when Simon told him he'd been asked to head the Illinois group. That was in 1975, two years after the baby murderers had persuaded the family haters on the Supreme Court to give women all over America abortion on demand.

Leave politics to the politicians, the old man had said. You got enough to do looking after your own family. Then he died before Simon's picture appeared in *Newsweek*. Died before Simon got the invitation to address the House of Bishops. He'd have seen that Simon truly was a rock, the rock on which a whole nation of Christians was building its hope of bringing morality back to America. Yes, Simon Peter, on this rock I will build my church. His daddy picked him to be the rock because he was the oldest and the younger ones had to obey him just like he had to obey his daddy. But sometimes the old man had his doubts. If only he could have lived to see this night.

Simon's heart started thudding faster and louder as he thought of the praise that lay ahead for him. Although the steak was cut thick and cooked the way he liked it, just a little pink showing, he could hardly taste it for excitement. But he politely handed sour cream to the bishop and glanced at Louise to make sure she was talking to the state representative on her left. He'd tried to impress on her before they left home how important it was to pay attention to the man, how much Simon needed him to carry out his program for Illinois, how she couldn't do her usual trick of staring at her plate all through dinner.

When she saw him looking at her she flushed and put down her fork and blurted something to her dinner partner. Simon shook his head a little, but nothing could really dampen his exultation. And it wasn't fair to her, not really; she wasn't at home with crowds and speeches as he was. She seldom came with him to public events. She didn't like to leave the children, even now that Tommy was eight and could get along without her.

He turned back to the bishop and delivered a short lecture on tactics in response to a comment the prelate had made with the sour cream.

'Of course it's largely a social problem,' the bishop said when Simon finished. 'The breakdown of the family. Parents unwilling to assume any moral authority. Very few with your kind of family-centered life. But you don't need me to tell you that.'

'It's a question of respect,' Simon said. 'Children don't respect their parents and their parents don't do anything to force them to. It was different when you and I were boys. You take my old man. You said "yessir" when you spoke to him or he made sure you never forgot a second time.'

The bishop smiled in polite agreement and told a long tale about the demoralized state of modern seminary training. Simon took another roll and explained that his daddy had been tough. Tough, but fair. He'd sometimes felt hurt when he was little, but now he thanked God he had a father like that, one who knew right from wrong and wouldn't put up with any crap. Nosir, you thought you were being 43 slick, putting one over the old man, but he was always a jump ahead of you. Had a hand as strong as a board. He wasn't afraid to use it, not even when you got to be as big as him. Bigger.

The bishop nodded and shared an anecdote about the man he'd first served under as a priest.

Simon pursed his lips and shook his head at the right places. That time he'd gone out drinking with his buddies, he'd been eighteen, getting ready to start at St Xavier's (stay with the Jesuits, his daddy said; they don't snivel every time some JD comes to them with a hard-luck story). He'd thought he was old enough to do what he wanted on Saturday night.

Don't be a sissy, for Christ's sake. He was pretty sure it was Jimmy who had put it into words, Jimmy who was going into the army along with Bobby Lee Andrews. That was when being a soldier meant something, not like now, when all the soft liberals in Congress encourage kids to burn their own country's flag. So he and Jimmy and Bobby went out with Carl and Joe. One last get-together for the team before they went their separate ways. The other guys were always on him, how he was scared of his old man. They didn't recognize it was respect, not fear.

You respect the man who's strong enough to know right from wrong and teach it to you.

But just that one time he couldn't take their hassling any more. He got weak, soft, caved in and went out with them. And then two in the morning, giggling drunk, trying to sneak in through the back door. His mother had left the back door open. She knew he was up to something so she snuck down and unlocked it. She was always soft, always weak, trying to subvert his daddy's strength. His father made rules and she tried to break them, but she couldn't. Nosir, not any more than her children. If she was fifteen dollars shy in the grocery money his daddy knew: he added all the bills against her household allowance. Don't tell me you lost a receipt, Marie, because I sure as hell don't believe you. Where'd that money go to, anyway? And she'd snuffle around and cry and try to lie, but his daddy could always tell.

It was disgusting watching her cry; it made him sick even to this day when he thought about it. He'd told Louise that back the first year they were married. Don't ever cry in front of your children, he warned her. At least, I'd better not ever hear of you doing it.

'The trouble is,' he said to the bishop, 'too many   45

men just are too lazy or too scared to buck all these libbers and liberals and take on their role as head of the family. They'd just as soon the government or the schools or someone did it for them. That's why you get all these girls going into the aborturaries and letting someone murder their babies. Their daddies or their husbands are just too damned – excuse me, Your Grace – too darned lazy to control them.'

The bishop smiled again, as if he was used to hearing people swear and used to hearing them apologize for it.

Simon's glow of satisfaction extended to his well-run family. None of his five daughters ever talked back to him. None of them had ever even tried, except Sandra. She was the oldest; maybe she thought that gave her special status, but he'd sure as hell beaten that nonsense out of her.

He didn't believe it when she was born. When the nurse came out and told him it was a girl he knew she'd made a mistake, confused him with one of the other men waiting for news. His daddy'd been so disappointed. Disappointed but pleased at the same time: it proved he was a bigger man than Simon would ever be. Then it had taken three more tries

before they got their first boy and he was a skinny

little runt, took after Louise's family. And then his daddy died before they got their second boy. They named him Tom for his grandpa, and he looked like him, a big, muscly boy, but it was too late; his daddy never saw Simon had finally gotten himself a real little man.

He realized he'd missed the bishop's next remark, but it didn't matter: he'd had the same conversation a hundred times and could respond without thinking. Not like the first time he'd talked to a bishop. Really talked, face to face, not just a handshake after a special service. He'd been so nervous his voice had come out in a little squeak, that high squeak he'd hated because it was how he always ended up sounding if he tried to argue with his daddy. But now he could see the bishops were men just like him, with the same kind of problems running their dioceses he had running his organization. Except now that he was head of the thing for the whole country it was probably more like being pope. Of course he never said any of this to the bishops, but it did give him a little edge over the man on his right. Just a suffragen, an assistant. Maybe twenty parishes under his care. Not like being responsible for the whole country.

The waitress filled Simon's coffee cup. He took

cream and sugar from the bishop and used them generously. When he turned to offer them to Louise he saw she'd already been given some by the state representative. She shouldn't use so much sugar; she'd never really gotten her figure back after Tommy was born. But he wasn't going to spoil his big night by worrying about her problems.

As the bishop finished his dessert Simon's heart started its happy thudding once more. The bishop deliberately folded his napkin in threes across the diagonal and put it on the table so it was exactly parallel with his plate. He waited for the master of ceremonies to inform the diners that they would have grace after dinner, then slowly stood and offered the benediction.

Simon fixed a pleased but humble look under his beard. He leaned over to the bishop when he sat down and made a jovial little comment. The bishop nodded and chuckled and everyone on the floor could see that Simon was on equal, maybe even superior terms, with a bishop.

The master of ceremonies told everyone how happy he was they could be here to honor Simon. A staunch fighter for the unborn . . . Untold thousands 48 of lives saved because of him . . . Wouldn't rest until babies were safe all over America . . . Special tribute tonight . . . But first they'd prepared a slide show: The Fight to Protect the Unborn.

The lights in the ballroom were dimmed and a screen unfolded on the stage behind the head table. Simon and the bishop turned their chairs around so they could see. After a second's hesitation, in which she looked first at Simon, then the state representative, Louise scooted around as well.

Simon had seen portions of the slide show before, sections that were used at fund-raising events and which showed him shaking hands with the President after their historic March for Life at the nation's capital. But they'd put that part together with a series taken at demonstrations and other important events around the country and added a soundtrack. The whole show had been completed in time for tonight's dinner. They'd use it in the future to educate high-school students and church groups on how to fight for Life, but it was being unveiled tonight just for him.

Their logo flashed on the screen while solemn but cheerful music played behind it. The dove of the Holy Spirit spreading its wings over the curled form of a helpless fetus. Then his own voice, his 49 well-practiced tenor that he'd spent four years in college studying speech to perfect, to get rid of that shameful squeak. It was a clip from the talk he'd made in Washington, the warm tones vibrating with emotion as he told the gathered hosts that no one in America could be free until every unborn life in America was held sacred.

While they played the speech, pictures flashed on the screen showing the mass of Pro-Life marchers carrying banners, holding up crosses to which they'd nailed cut-outs of murdered babies, all the marchers looking ardently at Simon, some with tears of shared passion in their eyes. Even now, six years later, listening to his own words his throat tightened again with rage felt on behalf of those million and a half babies murdered every year. Hands as big as his father's coming down to choke the life out of them. Even when he'd been eighteen, old enough to go to college, he hadn't been big enough to stand up to the old man, so how could a poor helpless baby in the womb who didn't have any hands at all stand up for itself?

The show went on to display pictures of Pro-Life activists marching outside death camps. Cheers came from the audience when the photo of a fire-bombed death chamber was projected on the screen. They'd have to take that one out when they showed it to the high-school students, but it proved that the helpless could gain power if they banded together.

The camera zoomed in close to the face of a girl going into one of the camps as she passed a line of peaceful picketers trying to get her to change her mind. Her face was soft, weak, scared.

Simon's fists clenched in his lap. Something about the girl made him think of his own mother. When his father beat him, her face had that same expression, frightened but withdrawn, a bystander at the torment of her own baby. Don't do it, Thomas, she would beg, tears streaming down her face. He couldn't stand to hear her crying, as if she was the one being punished, and all the candy hearts she gave him later never really soothed him. He never let Louise cry. She'd done it the first time he'd had to give Sandra a whipping for talking back to him. She'd come to him sobbing as if being weak and scared was any way to stop him teaching his children right from wrong. He'd made it real clear she was never to do it again.

Then the girl in the picture was shown changing her mind. The Pro-Life counselor was able to persuade her to put Life above her own selfish desires 51 to control her body. The audience cheered again as the girl walked off with the counselor to a Pro-Life clinic, funded with donations by tens of thousands of little people just like them who cared enough for Life to donate a few dollars every week.

Simon's fists relaxed and his mind wandered off to the remarks he'd make when his turn came. He'd worked on them all week, while flying to Toronto to protest the suspension of a policeman who wouldn't stand guard outside a death camp, while meeting in Springfield with key legislators on a number of bills to protect the unborn. He wanted to sound spontaneous, but authoritative, a leader people could rely on to make the right decisions.

Next to him Louise sucked in her breath, a little half-conscious sound of consternation. He glanced at her, then to the screen where she was staring. The picture showed a small band of picketers who faithfully came every Saturday to an abortuary in De Kalb. The soundtrack described how a few faithful could fight death and selfishness just as much as a big group could: the key was commitment. The Pro-Life counselor was exhorting a girl in a lime-green parka as she headed up the path to the death chamber

entrance.

Each shot moved in closer to the head bent in fear and weakness. Simon knew this face without seeing, knew it by the color of the parka, by the way the fine brown hair parted over the bowed white neck. His bowels were softening and turning over and his throat was so dry he could only trust himself to whisper.

'You did this,' he hissed to Louise under the flow of the soundtrack. She shook her head dumbly. 'You knew about this. You knew about this and never told me.' She only shook her head again, her eyes filled with tears. She turned to grab her napkin, turned so fast that she jarred the table and knocked a glass of water down the state representative's back.

The accident made her throat work with suppressed hysteria as she tried wiping her face, then the legislator's back. The state representative was gracious, helping to mop the front of her dress, laughing off the damp patch on his back, but Simon was sure he would be chuckling about him with other colleagues before the week was over: why should we listen to Simon? He can't even control his own wife.

Simon grabbed Louise's left arm and pulled her head down close to his mouth. 'You go off to the ladies' room,' he ordered in that same voiceless hiss. 'You leave now and don't come back until I'm through with my speech, you hear?'

Dumbly she pulled her arm away, apologizing through her tears to the state representative, dropping her handbag, spilling lipstick and Kleenex on the man's lap. The legislator patted her on the shoulder, tried to make out that he didn't mind, that it was an accident and he didn't need her to dry his back or pay to have his suit cleaned. She gave the man a fixed little smile and stumbled from the stage. If she'd practiced for a month she couldn't have done more to humiliate him.

The bishop leaned over and asked with unctuous concern if Louise was all right. Simon managed a twisted smile.

'She's fine. Just needs to go to the ladies'.'

But he could kill her for this. Kill her for destroying him at his moment of triumph, for working hand in glove with the old man to get him. He really thought he'd die. That night he came home drunk from being out with his buddies and his daddy stood waiting by the refrigerator with a baseball bat.

You tell me one reason why I shouldn't use this on you, Simon Peter. The rock. The old man spat at him. The sand. I'm like a man who built his house on the sand. And Simon tried talking to him, tried making his voice come out big and booming to say he was a man, he could go out with his buddies if he wanted, but the only thing that came out was that terrible little squeak and then the old man was hitting him, hitting him so hard he ended up on the floor, peeing in his pants. He was lying on the floor all wet and bleeding and sobbing while his mother stood crying at the top of the stairs, her tiny voice pleading for him from the distance.

And all the while Sandra's silhouette mocked him from the screen. 'One of our failures,' the sound-track intoned. 'We didn't have the resources to give this girl the help she needed to choose Life. But with your support we'll be able to help other girls like this one, so that truly every life in this great land of ours will be held sacred.'

MARTIN AMIS · *God's Dice*
HANS CHRISTIAN ANDERSEN · *The Emperor's New Clothes*
MARCUS AURELIUS · *Meditations*
JAMES BALDWIN · *Sonny's Blues*
AMBROSE BIERCE · *An Occurrence at Owl Creek Bridge*
DIRK BOGARDE · *From Le Pigeonnier*
WILLIAM BOYD · *Killing Lizards*
POPPY Z. BRITE · *His Mouth will Taste of Wormwood*
ITALO CALVINO · *Ten Italian Folktales*
ALBERT CAMUS · *Summer*
TRUMAN CAPOTE · *First and Last*
RAYMOND CHANDLER · *Goldfish*
ANTON CHEKHOV · *The Black Monk*
ROALD DAHL · *Lamb to the Slaughter*
ELIZABETH DAVID · *I'll be with You in the Squeezing of a Lemon*
N. J. DAWOOD (TRANS.) · *The Seven Voyages of Sindbad the Sailor*
ISAK DINESEN · *The Dreaming Child*
SIR ARTHUR CONAN DOYLE · *The Man with the Twisted Lip*
DICK FRANCIS · *Racing Classics*
SIGMUND FREUD · *Five Lectures on Psycho-Analysis*
KAHLIL GIBRAN · *Prophet, Madman, Wanderer*
STEPHEN JAY GOULD · *Adam's Navel*
ALASDAIR GRAY · *Five Letters from an Eastern Empire*
GRAHAM GREENE · *Under the Garden*
JAMES HERRIOT · *Seven Yorkshire Tales*
PATRICIA HIGHSMITH · *Little Tales of Misogyny*
M. R. JAMES AND R. L. STEVENSON · *The Haunted Dolls' House*
RUDYARD KIPLING · *Baa Baa, Black Sheep*
PENELOPE LIVELY · *A Long Night at Abu Simbel*
KATHERINE MANSFIELD · *The Escape*

GABRIEL GARCÍA MÁRQUEZ · *Bon Voyage, Mr President*
PATRICK MCGRATH · *The Angel*
HERMAN MELVILLE · *Bartleby*
SPIKE MILLIGAN · *Gunner Milligan, 954024*
MICHEL DE MONTAIGNE · *Four Essays*
JAN MORRIS · *From the Four Corners*
JOHN MORTIMER · *Rumpole and the Younger Generation*
R. K. NARAYAN · *Tales from Malgudi*
ANAIS NIN · *A Model*
FRANK O'CONNOR · *The Genius*
GEORGE ORWELL · *Pages from a Scullion's Diary*
CAMILLE PAGLIA · *Sex and Violence, or Nature and Art*
SARA PARETSKY · *A Taste of Life*
EDGAR ALLAN POE · *The Pit and the Pendulum*
MISS READ · *Village Christmas*
JEAN RHYS · *Let Them Call It Jazz*
DAMON RUNYON · *The Snatching of Bookie Bob*
SAKI · *The Secret Sin of Septimus Brope*
WILL SELF · *Scale*
GEORGES SIMENON · *Death of a Nobody*
MURIEL SPARK · *The Portobello Road*
ROBERT LOUIS STEVENSON · *The Pavilion on the Links*
PAUL THEROUX · *Down the Yangtze*
WILLIAM TREVOR · *Matilda's England*
MARK TULLY · *Ram Chander's Story*
JOHN UPDIKE · *Friends from Philadelphia*
EUDORA WELTY · *Why I Live at the P. O.*
EDITH WHARTON · *Madame de Treymes*
OSCAR WILDE · *The Happy Prince*
VIRGINIA WOOLF · *Killing the Angel in the House*

For complete information about books available from Penguin and how to order them, please write to us at the appropriate address below. Please note that for copyright reasons the selection of books varies from country to country.

IN THE UNITED KINGDOM: Please write to *Dept. JC, Penguin Books Ltd, FREEPOST, West Drayton, Middlesex UB7 0BR.*
If you have any difficulty in obtaining a title, please send your order with the correct money, plus ten per cent for postage and packaging, to *PO Box No. 11, West Drayton, Middlesex UB7 0BR.*

IN THE UNITED STATES: Please write to *Consumer Sales, Penguin USA, P.O. Box 999, Dept. 17109, Bergenfield, New Jersey 07621-0120.* VISA and MasterCard holders call 1-800-253-6476 to order all Penguin titles.

IN CANADA: Please write to *Penguin Books Canada Ltd, 10 Alcorn Avenue, Suite 300, Toronto, Ontario M4V 3B2.*

IN AUSTRALIA: Please write to *Penguin Books Australia Ltd, P.O. Box 257, Ringwood, Victoria 3134.*

IN NEW ZEALAND: Please write to *Penguin Books (NZ) Ltd, Private Bag 102902, North Shore Mail Centre, Auckland 10.*

IN INDIA: Please write to *Penguin Books India Pvt Ltd, 706 Eros Apartments, 56 Nehru Place, New Delhi 110 019.*

IN THE NETHERLANDS: Please write to *Penguin Books Netherlands bv, Postbus 3507, NL-1001 AH Amsterdam.*

IN GERMANY: Please write to *Penguin Books Deutschland GmbH, Metzlerstrasse 26, 60594 Frankfurt am Main.*

IN SPAIN: Please write to *Penguin Books S. A., Bravo Murillo 19, 1o B, 28015 Madrid.*

IN ITALY: Please write to *Penguin Italia s.r.l., Via Felice Casati 20, I-20124 Milano.*

IN FRANCE: Please write to *Penguin France S. A., 17 rue Lejeune, F-31000 Toulouse.*

IN JAPAN: Please write to *Penguin Books Japan, Ishikiribashi Building, 2-5-4, Suido, Bunkyo-ku, Tokyo 112.*

IN GREECE: Please write to *Penguin Hellas Ltd, Dimocritou 3, GR-106 71 Athens.*

IN SOUTH AFRICA: Please write to *Longman Penguin Southern Africa (Pty) Ltd, Private Bag X08, Bertsham 2013.*